D1119121

THIS CANDLEWICK BOOK BELONGS TO:

_____

_____

_____

_____

*For Barbara, who makes bears*
S.H.

*For Edward (Teddy) Craig*
H.C.

Text copyright © 1986 by Sarah Hayes
Illustrations copyright © 1986 by Helen Craig

Second U.S. paperback edition 1994
First published in Great Britain in 1986 by Walker Books Ltd., London.

Library of Congress Cataloging-in-Publication Data

Hayes, Sarah
This is the bear / written by Sarah Hayes ; illustrated
by Helen Craig.—2nd U.S. ed.
Summary: A toy bear is accidentally taken to the dump,
but is rescued by a boy and a dog.
ISBN 1-56402-189-0 (hardcover)
[1. Teddy bears—Fiction.  2. Stories in rhyme.]
I. Craig, Helen, ill. II. Title.
PZ8.3.H324Th  1993                92-53421
[E]—dc20
ISBN 1-56402-270-6 (paperback)

10 9 8 7 6 5 4

Printed in Hong Kong

The pictures for this book were done in watercolor and ink.

Candlewick Press
2067 Massachusetts Avenue
Cambridge, Massachusetts 02140

# — THIS IS THE —
# BEAR

by
## Sarah Hayes

illustrated by
## Helen Craig

CANDLEWICK PRESS
CAMBRIDGE, MASSACHUSETTS

This is the bear
who fell in the bin.

This is the dog
who pushed him in.

This is the man
who picked up the sack.

This is the driver
who would not come back.

# This is the bear
# who went to the dump

and fell on the pile
with a bit of a bump.

# This is the boy
# who took the bus

and went to the dump
to make a fuss.

This is the man
in an awful grump

who searched
and searched
and searched the dump.

# This is the bear
# all cold and cross

who never thought
he was really lost.

This is the dog

who smelled the smell

of a bone

and a can

and a bear as well.

This is the man
who drove them home –

the boy, the bear,
and the dog with a bone.

# This is the bear
# neat as a pin

who would not say
just where he had been.

This is the boy
who knew quite well,

but promised his friend
he would not tell.

And this is the boy
who woke up in the night
and asked the bear
if he felt all right –
and was very surprised
when the bear gave a shout,
"How soon can we have
another day out?"

SARAH HAYES worked in publishing and then as a free-lance writer and editor before beginning her career as a children's book author. She has written nearly twenty books for children, including two more books in this series, *This Is the Bear and the Picnic Lunch* and *This Is the Bear and the Scary Night*, as well as *The Cats of Tiffany Street*, and *Crumbling Castle*. Sarah lives with her husband and three children in Oxfordshire, England.

HELEN CRAIG worked as a commercial photographer for more than ten years before she began drawing and sculpting. Since her first children's book was published in 1970, she has illustrated more than thirty books for children, including the Angelina Ballerina books by Katharine Holabird, the This Is the Bear books by Sarah Hayes, and her own retelling of *The Town Mouse and the Country Mouse*. Helen Craig lives in Buckinghamshire, England.